The Berenstain Bears®
BACK TO SCHOOL

Stan & Jan Berenstain

GT
PUBLISHING

The members of the Bear family were sitting
around talking about their favorite things —

their favorite colors,

their favorite foods,

their favorite movies and
TV shows.

After a while they got to their favorite seasons. "What's your favorite season, Papa?" asked Brother.

"Winter," said Papa. "Winter is my favorite season because it's rugged.

I like the crunch of snow beneath my feet,

the little clouds your breath makes,

the beauty of snow in the forest. Yes, my favorite season is definitely winter."

"Tell me, cubs," said Papa. "What's your favorite season?"

"Summer!" shouted the cubs. It wasn't exactly a big surprise that summer was the cubs' favorite season.

Summer with its trips to the old swimming hole,

its overnight campouts,

and just lying around watching the sky.

"I bet I know your favorite season, Mama,"
said Sister. "Spring!"

"Well," said Mama, "I do like spring.
I like the spring flowers, and spring *is*
the best season for rainbows. But spring
isn't my favorite season. My favorite
season is fall."

"Why is that, Mama?" asked Brother.

"Is it because the leaves turn beautiful colors?" asked Sister.

"Is it because of October's bright blue weather?" asked Brother.

"No," said Mama. "Fall is my favorite season because in the fall, it's BACK TO SCHOOL!"

School! thought the cubs. They had
all but forgotten about school.

Their minds flashed back to the
last day of school, many weeks ago,
when they and their friends cheered, and
shouted, "No more pencils! No more books!
No more teacher's dirty looks!"

But soon they would be going
back to school and it would be,
"Lots more pencils! Lots more books!
Lots more teacher's dirty looks!"

Mama went to the calendar and circled the day they would be going back to school. Her thoughts were different.

Her thoughts were about putting her feet up and having a second cup of coffee after the big yellow school bus took the cubs off to school.

Perhaps she would catch up on her soap operas.

Maybe she would
do some shopping
at the mall.

As back-to-school day came closer,
the cubs began to worry.

"What if my new
teacher is a sourpuss
and doesn't like me?"
said Sister.

"What if I go out for soccer
and don't make the team?"
said Brother.

"What if the work is too hard and I can't do it?" said Sister.

"What if I get in trouble and get sent to the principal?" said Brother.

"Now, now," said Mama. "None of those things is going to happen. You're going to do fine."

"Your mama's right," said Papa. "There's absolutely nothing to worry about."

But the cubs couldn't help worrying. They were still worrying when the bus came and took them off to school.

Mama sighed as she
watched the school bus
disappear around the bend.

Woodsbear Papa had already
left for his work in the forest.

Alone at last, thought Mama
as she looked around the house.

She poured herself a second
cup of coffee and looked at
the morning paper. The headline
said: "School Starts Today!"
She already knew that.

Bear Country News
"School Starts Today!"

She put on one of her soap operas.
But it seemed stupid and boring,
and she had lost track of the story.

She decided to go shopping
at the mall. But by the time
she got ready, she had changed
her mind. She just wasn't in the
mood for shopping.

Sister's new teacher didn't turn out to be a sourpuss at all.

Nor was the work too hard.

The coach told Brother he was a sure starter on the soccer team.

And he did get sent to the principal — but it wasn't because he was in trouble. It was because he was chosen to be the principal's special messenger.

Mama was waiting when the school bus slowed to a stop and let Brother and Sister off.

"What was school like?" asked Mama.

"It was like... school," said Sister.

"What was the work like?" asked Mama.

"It was like... work," said Brother. "Hey!" he said as Mama picked up the cubs and gave them a really big hug.

"Hey!" said Sister. "We're just getting home from school is all, Mama!"

"Mmm!" said Brother. "I smell fresh-baked chocolate chip cookies!" The cubs ran into the kitchen, where fresh-baked chocolate chip cookies and tall glasses of cold milk awaited them.

"Mmm!" said Sister. "These cookies are good!"

"Glad you like them," said Mama.